Cobra Cat

Written by Tony Langham
Illustrated by Lynne Willey

Heinemann

Chapter 1

Tabitha was a travelling cat. She was always on the move. She was always looking for new places to go and new people to see.

One day Tabitha got on a big lorry without anyone seeing her and went all the way to India.

The lorry took Tabitha to a village.
The driver stopped to ask how to get
to the village shop. While he was
talking, Tabitha jumped down from
the back of the lorry and went off
to look around.

It was market day and it was very busy.
People were calling out all the things
they wanted to sell,
'Pots! Bananas! Mangoes! Chickens!'
Tabitha walked around the market.
She was very hungry and she went from
stall to stall hoping she would find
something to eat. She did not know that
someone was watching her.

5

It was a dog, one of the village dogs,
and it started to follow Tabitha.
Tabitha did not see the dog. She was
too busy trying to find something to eat.

Then another dog started to follow Tabitha. Then another, and another, until soon there were ten dogs, all following Tabitha around the market.

Suddenly Tabitha stopped. Something
told her that she was being followed.
She turned around. She saw a dog and
it growled at her. Then she saw all the
other dogs and they were growling too.

Tabitha started to run. The dogs started to chase her. Tabitha ran all over the market place. So did the dogs. Pots, bananas, mangoes and chickens flew everywhere.

Tabitha ran off down the street.
The dogs were getting nearer and
nearer all the time. Faster and faster
they ran. Then Tabitha saw a tree.
Just as the dogs were about to catch
her, Tabitha jumped. She quickly
climbed up the tree and on to a
high branch.

The dogs stopped under the tree and growled and growled. They tried to jump up, but Tabitha was too high up in the tree. Then suddenly all the dogs went quiet. Someone was shouting at them. It was a boy and he was waving a stick at them.

'Get away! Get away!' he shouted.

The dogs turned and ran away.
Only one big dog stopped and growled
at the boy. So the boy threw his stick
at the dog and then it ran off too.
When they were gone, the boy looked up
at Tabitha.

'You can come down now,' he said, and
Tabitha climbed down from the tree.

'Meow,' went Tabitha.

'You should be safe now,' said the boy,
and he turned and walked away.

But Tabitha started to follow him.

Chapter 2

Tabitha followed the boy back through the village. The boy went up a path to a house. Tabitha stopped and watched him. She saw a woman come out of the house.

'Hello Mother,' said the boy.

'Why are you so late, Pravin?' she asked.

'I stopped to help a cat,' said Pravin.

'Is that the cat?' asked his mother.

Pravin turned round and saw Tabitha sitting on the path.

Pravin told his mother what had
happened in the village.
'You did the right thing,' his mother
said, 'but she can't stay here.'
Pravin knew that. His family was very
poor and they never had much food to
eat. He looked at Tabitha.
'She will go away soon,' he said, and
he went inside the house.

But Tabitha did not go away.
She stayed in the garden all night.
When she woke up in the morning she
was very hungry so she went to find
some food. She was thinking of eating
a mouse.

She looked in the
vegetable garden.
Nothing there.

Then she looked
round the back
of the house.
Nothing there.

So Tabitha walked round the house again. Then she saw something sliding up the path. It was a snake, a big brown and yellow cobra. She saw the snake go into the house. Tabitha forgot how hungry she was and she followed the snake.

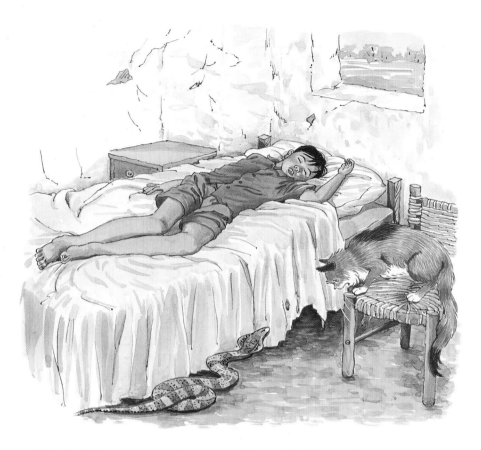

Tabitha saw the snake sliding into
a room and again she followed it.
There was a bed in the middle of the
room. The snake was sliding quietly
over to it. Tabitha jumped up on to
a chair. Then she saw who was in
the bed. It was Pravin.

The snake was getting nearer and
nearer to Pravin and Tabitha knew
she had to do something. She quickly
jumped from the chair and on to
the bed.

'MEOW! MEOW!' she went, and she
tried to make as much noise as she could.
Pravin woke up. He saw Tabitha and the
snake and shouted, 'Mother! Mother!
Come quickly! There's a snake!'

Pravin's mother ran into the room.
She was carrying a long brush.
Very carefully she lifted the snake
up with the brush and threw it out of
the window.

'It was the cat that woke me up,'
said Pravin. 'She saved me!'

'She is a very clever cat,' said his mother.

'Meow,' went Tabitha.

21

'She looks hungry,' said Pravin's mother.
'Would you like something to eat, cat?'
'Meow!' went Tabitha.
So Pravin and his mother took Tabitha
into the kitchen and gave her some milk.

'I think we could let her stay after all,'
said Pravin's mother.
'Did you hear that, cat?' asked Pravin.
'You would like that, wouldn't you?'

But when he
turned round
to look at Tabitha
she was not there.

Back in the village the driver of the lorry was getting back into his cab. He started the lorry and went back up the hill and out of the village. Riding in the back of the lorry was Tabitha. She never stayed in one place for long because Tabitha was a travelling cat.